D1498986

7/04

Millions of Americans remember Dick and Jane (and Sally and Spot too!). The little stories with their simple vocabulary words and warmly rendered illustrations were a hallmark of American education in the 1950s and 1960s.

But the first Dick and Jane stories actually appeared much earlier—in the Scott Foresman Elson Basic Reader Pre-Primer, copyright 1930. These books featured short, upbeat, and highly readable stories for children. The pages were filled with colorful characters and large, easy-to-read Century Schoolbook typeface. There were fun adventures around every corner of Dick and Jane's world.

Generations of American children learned to read with Dick and Jane, and many still cherish the memory of reading the simple stories on their own. Today, Pearson Scott Foresman remains committed to helping all children learn to read—and love to read. As part of Pearson Education, the world's largest educational publisher, Pearson Scott Foresman is honored to reissue these classic Dick and Jane stories, with Grosset & Dunlap, a division of Penguin Young Readers Group. Reading has always been at the heart of everything we do, and we sincerely hope that reading is an important part of your life too.

Library of Congress Cataloging-in-Publication Data
We play.
        p. cm. — (Read with Dick and Jane ; 11)
    Summary: A collection of classic Dick and Jane stories in which they run and play with
Sally, Spot, and their parents.
    ISBN 0-448-43410-5 (pbk.) — ISBN 0-448-43496-2 (hardcover)
    [1. Play—Fiction. 2. Pets—Fiction. 3. Vocabulary.] I. Series.
    PZ7.W35142 2004
    [E]—dc22   2003016831

ISBN 0-448-43496-2 (GB)   A B C D E F G H I J
ISBN 0-448-43410-5 (pbk)   A B C D E F G H I J

Read with
Dick and Jane

We Play

GROSSET & DUNLAP • NEW YORK

Table of Contents

Play

Oh, Father.
See funny Dick.
Dick can play.

Oh, Mother.
Oh, Father.
Jane can play.
Sally can play.

Oh, Father.
See Spot.
Funny, funny Spot.
Spot can play.

See Dick Play

Look, Jane.

Look, look.

Look and see.

See Father play.

See Dick play.

Look, Mother.
Look, Mother, look.
See Father.
See Father and Dick.

Oh, Mother.

See Spot.

Look, Mother, look.

Spot can help Dick.

Funny Spot

Come Spot.
Come, come.
Play Spot.
Play, play.

Go, Spot.

Go, go.

Spot can play.

Dick can play.

Oh, oh.
Funny, funny Spot.

See Spot Play

See Jane jump.

Jump, jump.

See Spot jump.

Jump, jump.

Oh, Dick.

Oh, Jane.

See Spot.

Funny, funny Spot.
Spot can play.

Funny Father

"Come, Jane," said Father.
"Come and play ball.
Come and play."

"I can help you play ball," said Father.
"I can help."

"Come, Father," said Jane.
"Come and play ball.
Come and play."

Oh, funny, funny Father.

Play Ball

"Come, Jane," said Father.
"Come and play ball.
Come and play."

"Oh," said Jane.
"See the red ball go.
See it go up, up, up.
Run, Dick, run."

"Oh, oh," said Dick.
"Where is my ball?
I can not find it.
Come here, Jane.
Run and help me.
Help me find my red ball."

"I can help you," said Jane.
"We can find the red ball."

Dick said, "I see it.
I see my red ball.
Look, Father.
See where it is.
Come and help me."

Jane said, "Oh, Dick.
Spot can help you.
Spot can find the ball."